Henry Van Dyke

The Lost Word - A Christmas Legend of Long ago

Henry Van Dyke

The Lost Word - A Christmas Legend of Long ago

ISBN/EAN: 9783337165390

Printed in Europe, USA, Canada, Australia, Japan

Cover: Foto ©Andreas Hilbeck / pixelio.de

More available books at **www.hansebooks.com**

BOOKS BY HENRY VAN DYKE, D.D.

THE LOST WORD

" He opened his heart to the old man and told him
the story of his life."

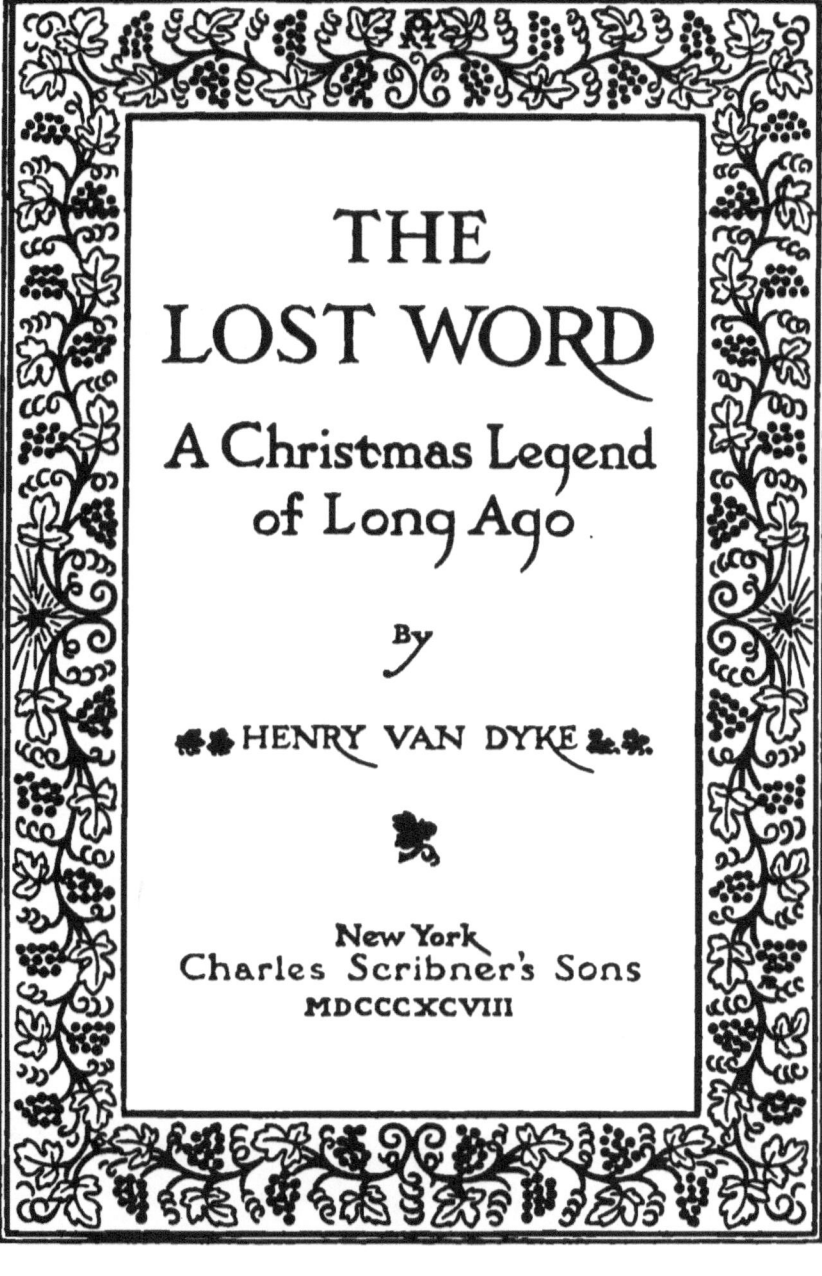

THE
LOST WORD

A Christmas Legend
of Long Ago

By

HENRY VAN DYKE

New York
Charles Scribner's Sons
MDCCCXCVIII

DEDICATED
TO MY FRIEND
HAMILTON W. MABIE

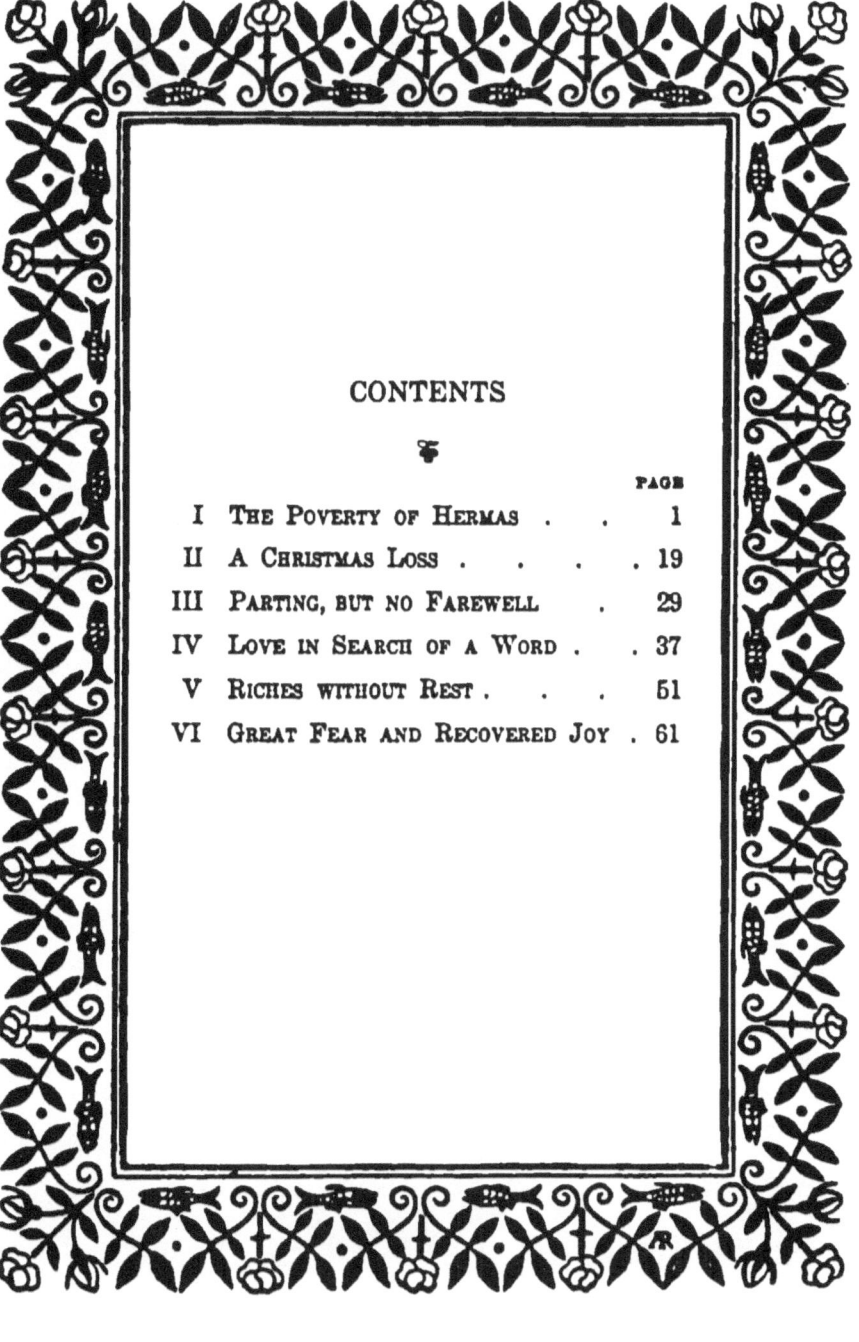

CONTENTS

		PAGE
I	THE POVERTY OF HERMAS	1
II	A CHRISTMAS LOSS	19
III	PARTING, BUT NO FAREWELL	29
IV	LOVE IN SEARCH OF A WORD	37
V	RICHES WITHOUT REST	51
VI	GREAT FEAR AND RECOVERED JOY	61

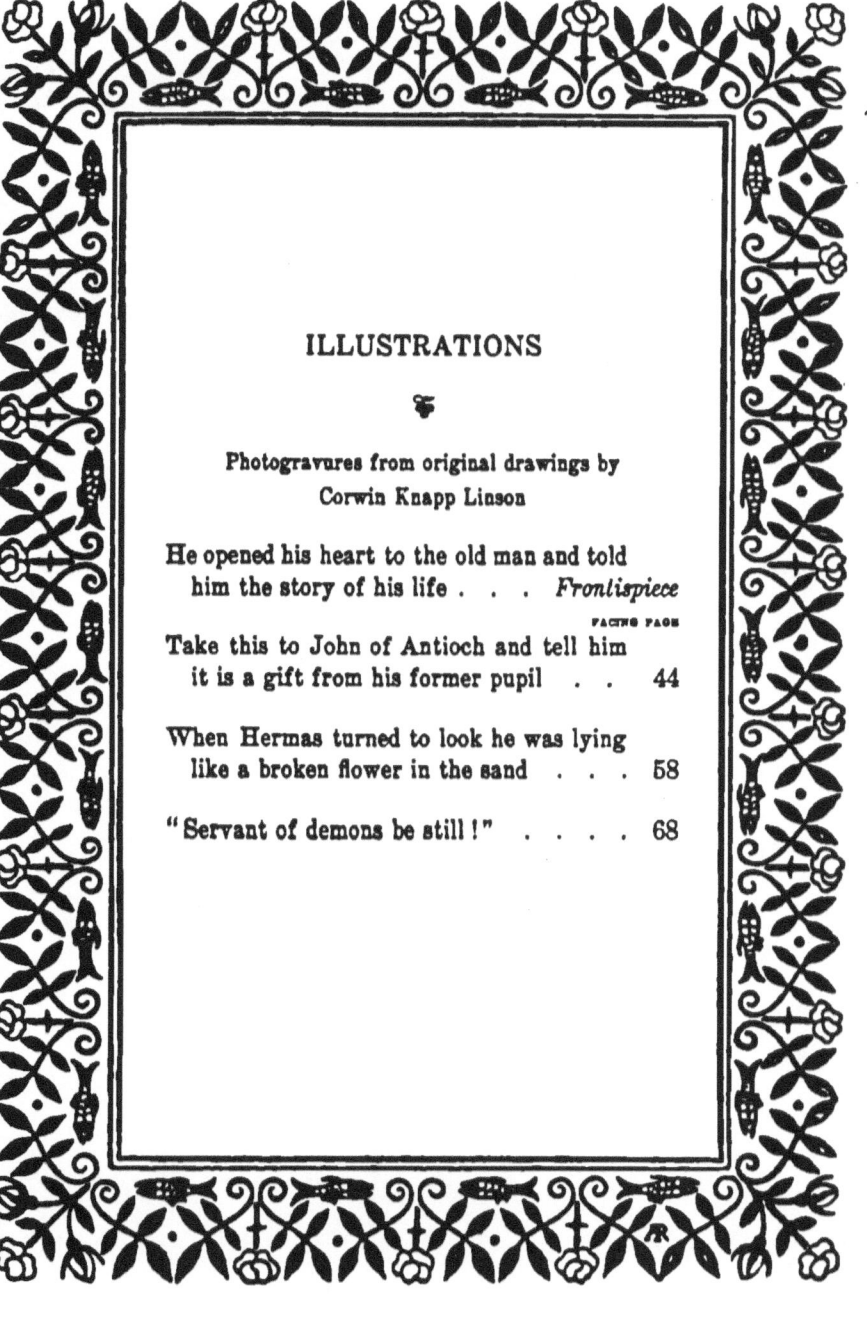

ILLUSTRATIONS

❦

Photogravures from original drawings by
Corwin Knapp Linson

He opened his heart to the old man and told
   him the story of his life . . . *Frontispiece*

FACING PAGE

Take this to John of Antioch and tell him
   it is a gift from his former pupil . . 44

When Hermas turned to look he was lying
   like a broken flower in the sand . . . 58

"Servant of demons be still!" 68

I

THE POVERTY OF HERMAS

I

"COME down, Hermas, come down! The night is past. It is time to be stirring. Christ is born to-day. Peace be with you in His name. Make haste and come down!"

A little group of young men were standing in a street of Antioch, in the dusk of early morning, fifteen hundred years ago. It was a class of candidates who had nearly finished their two years of training for the Christian church. They had come to call their fellow-student Hermas from his lodging.

Their voices rang out cheerily through the cool air. They were full of that glad sense of life which the young feel when

3

they awake and come to rouse one who is still sleeping. There was a note of friendly triumph in their call, as if they were exulting unconsciously in having begun the adventure of the new day before their comrade.

But Hermas was not asleep. He had been waking for hours, and the dark walls of his narrow lodging had been a prison to his restless heart. A nameless sorrow and discontent had fallen upon him, and he could find no escape from the heaviness of his own thoughts.

There is a sadness of youth into which the old cannot enter. It seems to them unreal and causeless. But it is even more bitter and burdensome than the sadness of age. There is a sting of resentment in it, a fever of angry surprise that the world should so soon be a disappointment, and life so early take on the look of a failure. It has little reason in it, perhaps, but it has all the more weariness and gloom, because the man who is oppressed by it feels dimly

4

that it is an unnatural and an unreasonable thing, that he should be separated from the joy of his companions, and tired of living before he has fairly begun to live.

Hermas had fallen into the very depths of this strange self-pity. He was out of tune with everything around him. He had been thinking, through the dead, still night, of all that he had given up when he left the house of his father, the wealthy pagan Demetrius, to join the company of the Christians. Only two years ago he had been one of the richest young men in Antioch. Now he was one of the poorest. And the worst of it was that, though he had made the choice willingly and accepted the sacrifice with a kind of enthusiasm, he was already dissatisfied with it.

The new life was no happier than the old. He was weary of vigils and fasts, weary of studies and penances, weary of prayers and sermons. He felt like a slave in a treadmill. He knew that he must go on. His honour, his conscience, his sense of duty,

5

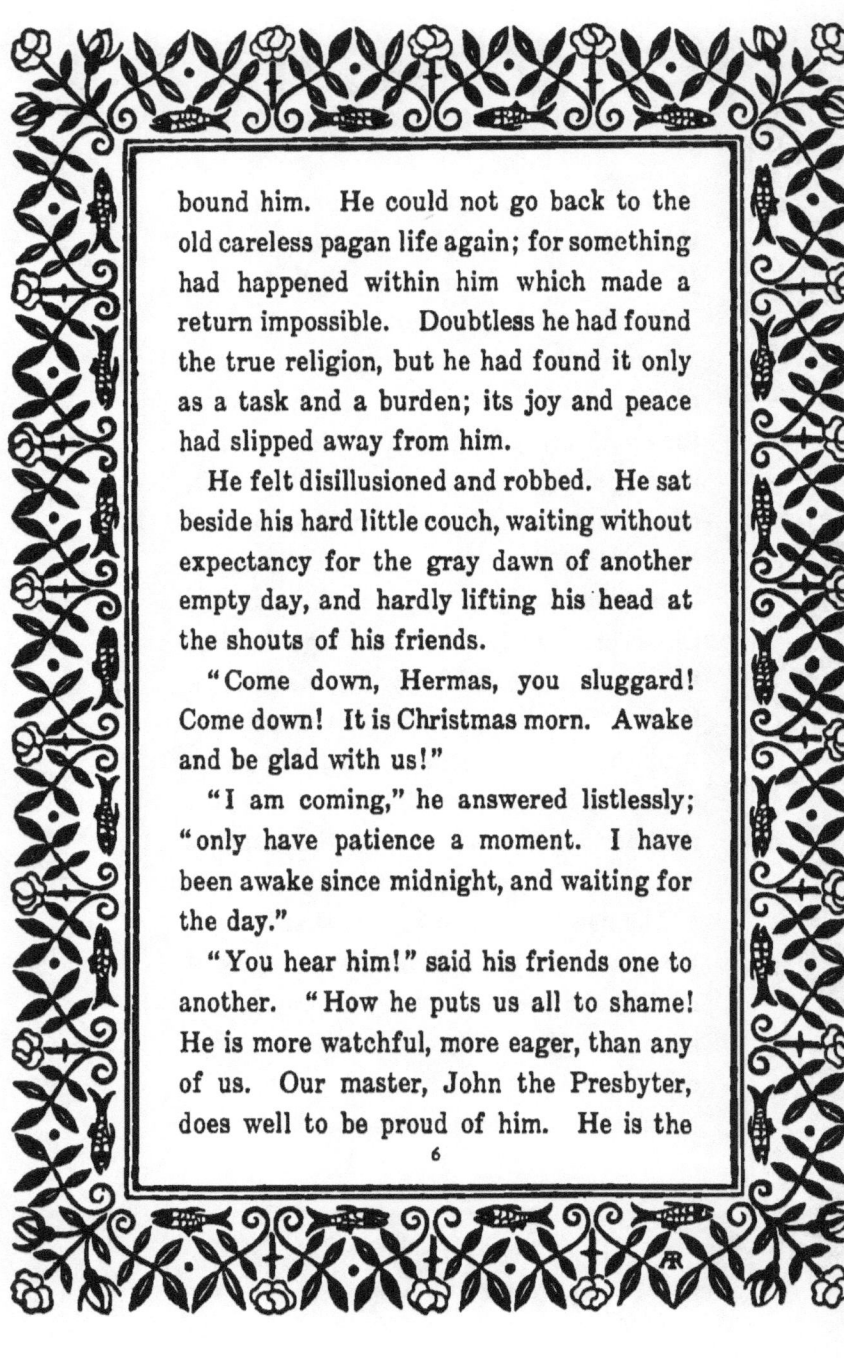

bound him. He could not go back to the old careless pagan life again; for something had happened within him which made a return impossible. Doubtless he had found the true religion, but he had found it only as a task and a burden; its joy and peace had slipped away from him.

He felt disillusioned and robbed. He sat beside his hard little couch, waiting without expectancy for the gray dawn of another empty day, and hardly lifting his head at the shouts of his friends.

"Come down, Hermas, you sluggard! Come down! It is Christmas morn. Awake and be glad with us!"

"I am coming," he answered listlessly; "only have patience a moment. I have been awake since midnight, and waiting for the day."

"You hear him!" said his friends one to another. "How he puts us all to shame! He is more watchful, more eager, than any of us. Our master, John the Presbyter, does well to be proud of him. He is the best man in our class. When he is baptized the church will get a strong member."

While they were talking the door opened and Hermas stepped out. He was a figure to be remarked in any company—tall, broad-shouldered, straight-hipped, with a head proudly poised on the firm column of the neck, and short brown curls clustering over the square forehead. It was the perpetual type of vigourous and intelligent young manhood, such as may be found in every century among the throngs of ordinary men, as if to show what the flower of the race should be. But the light in his dark blue eyes was clouded and uncertain; his smooth cheeks were leaner than they should have been at twenty; and there were downward lines about his mouth which spoke of desires unsatisfied and ambitions repressed. He joined his companions with brief greetings,—a nod to one, a word to another,—and they passed together down the steep street.

Overhead the mystery of daybreak was

silently transfiguring the sky. The curtain of darkness had lifted softly upward along the edge of the horizon. The ragged crests of Mount Silpius were outlined with pale rosy light. In the central vault of heaven a few large stars twinkled drowsily. The great city, still chiefly pagan, lay more than half asleep. But multitudes of the Christians, dressed in white and carrying lighted torches in their hands, were hurrying toward the Basilica of Constantine to keep the latest holy day of the church, the new festival of the birthday of their Master.

The vast, bare building was soon crowded, and the younger converts, who were not yet permitted to stand among the baptized, found it difficult to come to their appointed place between the first two pillars of the house, just within the threshold. There was some good-humoured pressing and jostling about the door; but the candidates pushed steadily forward.

"By your leave, friends, our station is

beyond you. Will you let us pass? Many thanks."

A touch here, a courteous nod there, a little patience, a little persistence, and at last they stood in their place. Hermas was taller than his companions; he could look easily over their heads and survey the white sea of people stretching away through the columns, under the shadows of the high roof, as the tide spreads on a calm day into the pillared cavern of Staffa, quiet as if the ocean hardly dared to breathe. The light of many flambeaux fell, in flickering, uncertain rays, over the assembly. At the end of the vista there was a circle of clearer, steadier radiance. Hermas could see the bishop in his great chair, surrounded by the presbyters, the lofty desks on either side for the readers of the Scripture, the communion-table and the table of offerings in the middle of the church.

The call to prayer sounded down the long aisle. Thousands of hands were joyously lifted in the air, as if the sea had blossomed

9

into waving lilies, and the "Amen" was like the murmur of countless ripples in an echoing place.

Then the singing began, led by the choir of a hundred trained voices which the Bishop Paul had founded in Antioch. Timidly, at first, the music felt its way, as the people joined with a broken and uncertain cadence, the mingling of many little waves not yet gathered into rhythm and harmony. Soon the longer, stronger billows of song rolled in, sweeping from side to side as the men and the women answered in the clear antiphony.

Hermas had often been carried on those

"Tides of music's golden sea
Setting toward eternity."

But to-day his heart was a rock that stood motionless. The flood passed by and left him unmoved.

Looking out from his place at the foot of the pillar, he saw a man standing far off in the lofty bema. Short and slender, wasted by sickness, gray before his time, with pale cheeks and wrinkled brow, he seemed at first like a person of no significance—a reed shaken in the wind. But there was a look in his deep-set, poignant eyes, as he gathered all the glances of the multitude to himself, that belied his mean appearance and prophesied power. Hermas knew very well who it was: the man who had drawn him from his father's house, the teacher who was instructing him as a son in the Christian faith, the guide and trainer of his soul—John of Antioch, whose fame filled the city and began to overflow Asia, and who was called already Chrysostom, the golden-mouthed preacher.

Hermas had felt the magic of his eloquence many a time; and to-day, as the tense voice vibrated through the stillness, and the sentences moved onward, growing fuller and stronger, bearing argosies of costly rhetoric and treasures of homely speech in their bosom, and drawing the hearts of men with a resistless magic,

Hermas knew that the preacher had never been more potent, more inspired.

He played on that immense congregation as a master on an instrument. He rebuked their sins, and they trembled. He touched their sorrows, and they wept. He spoke of the conflicts, the triumphs, the glories of their faith, and they broke out in thunders of applause. He hushed them into reverent silence, and led them tenderly, with the wise men of the East, to the lowly birth-place of Jesus.

"Do thou, therefore, likewise leave the Jewish people, the troubled city, the blood-thirsty tyrant, the pomp of the world, and hasten to Bethlehem, the sweet house of spiritual bread. For though thou be but a shepherd, and come hither, thou shalt behold the young Child in an inn. Though thou be a king, and come not hither, thy purple robe shall profit thee nothing. Though thou be one of the wise men, this shall be no hindrance to thee. Only let thy coming be to honour and adore, with trembling joy, the Son of God, to whose name be glory, on this His birthday, and forever and forever."

The soul of Hermas did not answer to the musician's touch. The strings of his heart were slack and soundless; there was no response within him. He was neither shepherd, nor king, nor wise man; only an unhappy, dissatisfied, questioning youth. He was out of sympathy with the eager preacher, the joyous hearers. In their harmony he had no part. Was it for this that he had forsaken his inheritance and narrowed his life to poverty and hardship? What was it all worth?

The gracious prayers with which the young converts were blessed and dismissed before the sacrament sounded hollow in his ears. Never had he felt so utterly lonely as in that praying throng. He went out with his companions like a man departing from a banquet where all but he had been fed.

"Farewell, Hermas," they cried, as he

turned from them at the door.   But he did
not look back, nor wave his hand.   He was
alone already in his heart.

When he entered the broad Avenue of the
Colonnades, the sun had already topped the
eastern hills, and the ruddy light was
streaming through the long double row of
archways and over the pavements of crim-
son marble.   But Hermas turned his back
to the morning, and walked with his shadow
before him.

The street began to swarm and whirl and
quiver with the motley life of a huge city:
beggars and jugglers, dancers and musi-
cians, gilded youths in their chariots, and
daughters of joy looking out from their
windows, all intoxicated with the mere delight of living and the gladness of a new
day.   The pagan populace of Antioch—
reckless, pleasure-loving, spendthrift—were
preparing for the Saturnalia.   But all this
Hermas had renounced.   He cleft his
way through the crowd slowly, like a re-

luctant swimmer weary of breasting the tide.

At the corner of the street where the narrow, populous Lane of the Camel-drivers crossed the Colonnades, a story-teller had bewitched a circle of people around him. It was the same old tale of love and adventure that many generations have listened to; but the lively fancy of the hearers lent it new interest, and the wit of the improviser drew forth sighs of interest and shouts of laughter.

A yellow-haired girl on the edge of the throng turned, as Hermas passed, and smiled in his face. She put out her hand and caught him by the sleeve.

"Stay," she said, "and laugh a bit with us. I know who you are—the son of Demetrius. You must have bags of gold. Why do you look so black? Love is alive yet."

Hermas shook off her hand, but not ungently.

"I don't know what you mean," he said.

15

"You are mistaken in me. I am poorer than you are."

But as he passed on, he felt the warm touch of her fingers through the cloth on his arm. It seemed as if she had plucked him by the heart.

He went out by the Western Gate, under the golden cherubim that the Emperor Titus had stolen from the ruined Temple of Jerusalem and fixed upon the arch of triumph. He turned to the left, and climbed the hill to the road that led to the Grove of Daphne.

In all the world there was no other highway as beautiful. It wound for five miles along the foot of the mountains, among gardens and villas, plantations of myrtles and mulberries, with wide outlooks over the valley of Orontes and the distant, shimmering sea.

The richest of all the dwellings was the House of the Golden Pillars, the mansion of Demetrius. He had won the favor of the apostate Emperor Julian, whose vain

16

efforts to restore the worship of the heathen gods, some twenty years ago, had opened an easy way to wealth and power for all who would mock and oppose Christianity. Demetrius was not a sincere fanatic like his royal master; but he was bitter enough in his professed scorn of the new religion, to make him a favourite at the court where the old religion was in fashion. He had reaped a rich reward of his policy, and a strange sense of consistency made him more fiercely loyal to it than if it had been a real faith. He was proud of being called "the friend of Julian"; and when his son joined himself to the Christians, and acknowledged the unseen God, it seemed like an insult to his father's success. He drove the boy from his door and disinherited him.

The glittering portico of the serene, haughty house, the repose of the well-ordered garden, still blooming with belated flowers, seemed at once to deride and to invite the young outcast plodding along the dusty road. "This is your birthright," whispered the clambering rose-trees by the gate; and the closed portals of carven bronze said: "You have sold it for a thought—a dream."

II

A CHRISTMAS LOSS

II

HERMAS found the Grove of Daphne quite deserted. There was no sound in the enchanted vale but the rustling of the light winds chasing each other through the laurel thickets, and the babble of innumerable streams. Memories of the days and nights of delicate pleasure that the grove had often seen still haunted the bewildered paths and broken fountains. At the foot of a rocky eminence, crowned with the ruins of Apollo's temple, which had been mysteriously destroyed by fire just after Julian had restored and reconsecrated it, Hermas sat down beside a gushing spring, and gave himself up to sadness.

"How beautiful the world would be, how

joyful, how easy to live in, without religion! These questions about unseen things, perhaps about unreal things, these restraints and duties and sacrifices—if I were only free from them all, and could only forget them all, then I could live my life as I pleased, and be happy."

"Why not?" said a quiet voice at his back.

He turned, and saw an old man with a long beard and a threadbare cloak (the garb affected by the pagan philosophers) standing behind him and smiling curiously.

"How is it that you answer that which has not been spoken?" said Hermas; "and who are you that honour me with your company?"

"Forgive the intrusion," answered the stranger; "it is not ill meant. A friendly interest is as good as an introduction."

"But to what singular circumstance do I owe this interest?"

"To your face," said the old man, with a courteous inclination. "Perhaps also a little to the fact that I am the oldest inhabitant here, and feel as if all visitors were my guests, in a way "

" Are you, then, one of the keepers of the grove? And have you given up your work with the trees to take a holiday as a philosopher?"

" Not at all. The robe of philosophy is a mere affectation, I must confess. I think little of it. My profession is the care of altars. In fact, I am that solitary priest of Apollo whom the Emperor Julian found here when he came to revive the worship of the grove, some twenty years ago. You have heard of the incident?"

" Yes," said Hermas, beginning to be interested; " the whole city must have heard of it, for it is still talked of. But surely it was a strange sacrifice that you brought to celebrate the restoration of Apollo's temple?"

" You mean the goose? Well, perhaps it was not precisely what the emperor expected. But it was all that I had, and it seemed to me not inappropriate. You will agree to that if you are a Christian, as I guess from your dress."

"You speak lightly for a priest of Apollo."

"Oh, as for that, I am no bigot. The priesthood is a professional matter, and the name of Apollo is as good as any other. How many altars do you think there have been in this grove?"

"I do not know."

"Just four-and-twenty, including that of the martyr Babylas, whose ruined chapel you see just beyond us. I have had something to do with most of them in my time. They are transitory. They give employment to care-takers for a while. But the thing that lasts, and the thing that interests me, is the human life that plays around them. The game has been going on for centuries. It still disports itself very pleasantly on summer evenings through these shady walks. Believe me, for I know. Daphne and Apollo were shadows. But the flying maidens and the pursuing lovers, the music and the dances, these are the realities. Life is the game, and the world keeps it up merrily. But you? You are of a sad countenance for one so young and so fair. Are you a loser in the game?"

The words and tone of the speaker fitted Hermas' mood as a key fits the lock. He opened his heart to the old man, and told him the story of his life: his luxurious boyhood in his father's house; the irresistible spell which compelled him to forsake it when he heard John's preaching of the new religion; his lonely year with the anchorites among the mountains; the strict discipline in his teacher's house at Antioch; his weariness of duty, his distaste for poverty, his discontent with worship.

"And to-day," said he, "I have been thinking that I am a fool. My life is swept as bare as a hermit's cell. There is nothing in it but a dream, a thought of God, which does not satisfy me."

The singular smile deepened on his companion's face. "You are ready, then," he suggested, "to renounce your new religion and go back to that of your father?"

"No; I renounce nothing, I accept nothing. I do not wish to think about it. I only wish to live."

"A very reasonable wish, and I think you are about to see its accomplishment. Indeed, I may even say that I can put you in the way of securing it. Do you believe in magic?"

"I have told you already that I do not know whether I believe in anything. This is not a day on which I care to make professions of faith. I believe in what I see. I want what will give me pleasure."

"Well," said the old man, soothingly, as he plucked a leaf from the laurel-tree above them and dipped it in the spring, "let us dismiss the riddles of belief. I like them as little as you do. You know this is a Castalian fountain. The Emperor Hadrian once read his fortune here from a leaf dipped in the water. Let us see what this

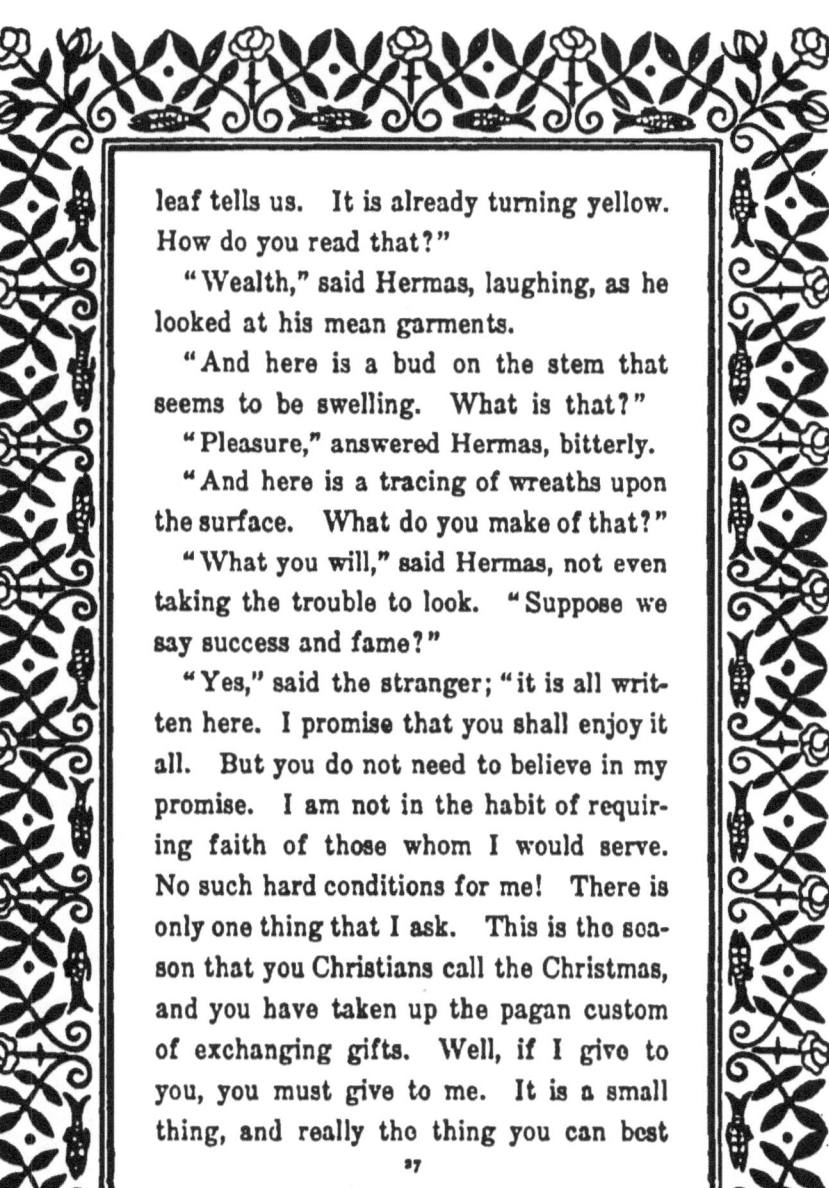

leaf tells us. It is already turning yellow. How do you read that?"

"Wealth," said Hermas, laughing, as he looked at his mean garments.

"And here is a bud on the stem that seems to be swelling. What is that?"

"Pleasure," answered Hermas, bitterly.

"And here is a tracing of wreaths upon the surface. What do you make of that?"

"What you will," said Hermas, not even taking the trouble to look. "Suppose we say success and fame?"

"Yes," said the stranger; "it is all written here. I promise that you shall enjoy it all. But you do not need to believe in my promise. I am not in the habit of requiring faith of those whom I would serve. No such hard conditions for me! There is only one thing that I ask. This is the season that you Christians call the Christmas, and you have taken up the pagan custom of exchanging gifts. Well, if I give to you, you must give to me. It is a small thing, and really the thing you can best afford to part with: a single word—the name of Him you profess to worship. Let me take that word and all that belongs to it entirely out of your life, so that you shall never need to hear it or speak it again. You will be richer without it. I promise you everything, and this is all I ask in return. Do you consent?"

"Yes, I consent," said Hermas, mocking. "If you can take your price, a word, you can keep your promise, a dream."

The stranger laid the long, cool, wet leaf softly across the young man's eyes. An icicle of pain darted through them; every nerve in his body was drawn together there in a knot of agony.

Then all the tangle of pain seemed to be lifted out of him. A cool languor of delight flowed back through every vein, and he sank into a profound sleep.

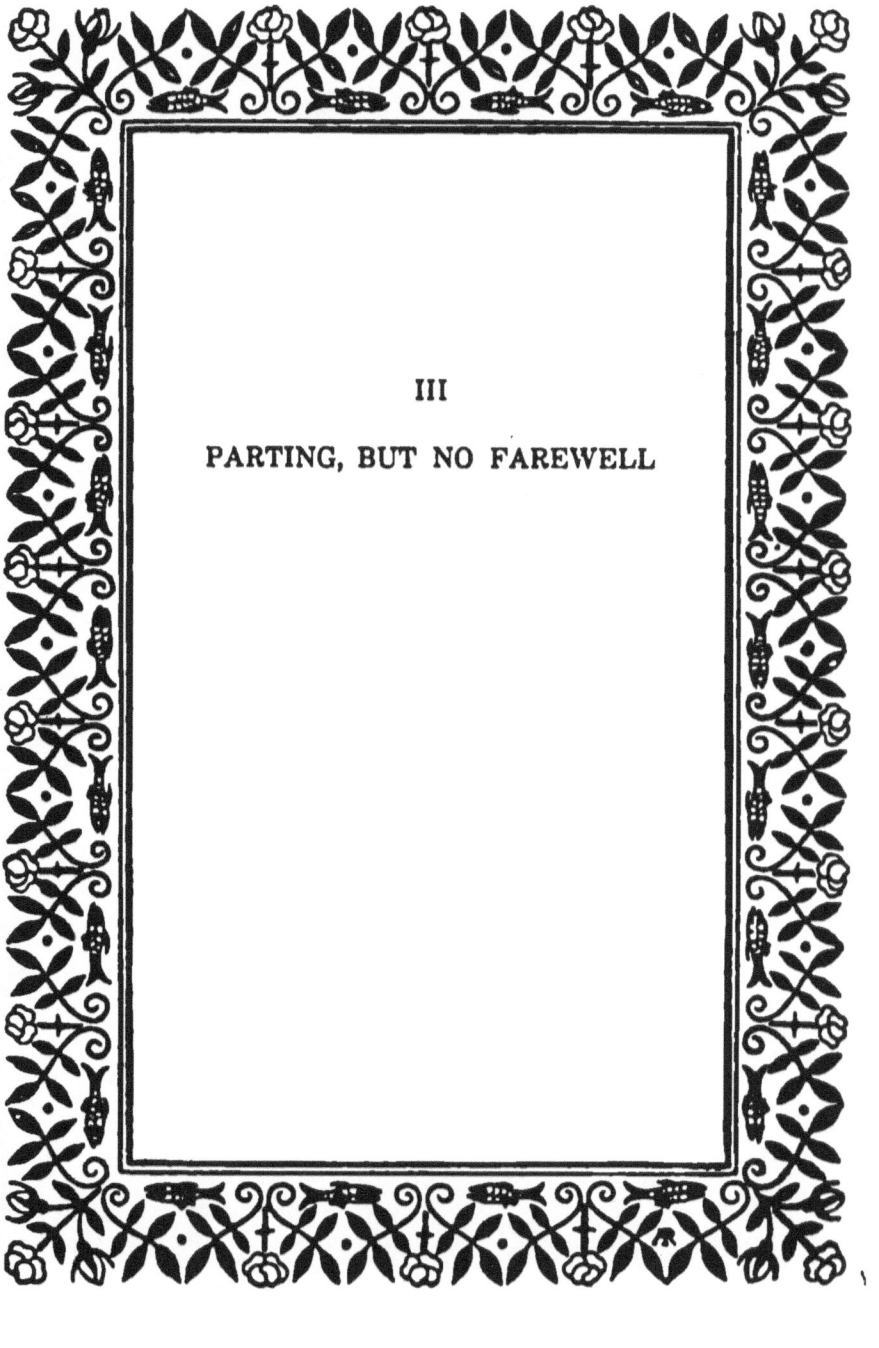

III

PARTING, BUT NO FAREWELL

III

THERE is a slumber so deep that it annihilates time. It is like a fragment of eternity. Beneath its enchantment of vacancy, a day seems like a thousand years, and a thousand years might well pass as one day.

It was such a sleep that fell upon Hermas in the Grove of Daphne. An immeasurable period, an interval of life so blank and empty that he could not tell whether it was long or short, had passed over him when his senses began to stir again. The setting sun was shooting arrows of gold under the glossy laurel-leaves. He rose and stretched his arms, grasping a smooth branch above him and shaking it, to make sure that he was alive. Then he hurried back toward Antioch, treading lightly as if on air.

The ground seemed to spring beneath his feet. Already his life had changed, he knew not how. Something that did not belong to him had dropped away; he had returned to a former state of being. He felt as if anything might happen to him, and he was ready for anything. He was a new man, yet curiously familiar to himself—as if he had done with playing a tiresome part and returned to his natural state. He was buoyant and free, without a care, a doubt, a fear.

As he drew near to his father's house he saw a confusion of servants in the porch, and the old steward ran down to meet him at the gate.

"Lord, we have been seeking you everywhere. The master is at the point of death, and has sent for you. Since the sixth hour he calls your name continually. Come to him quickly, lord, for I fear the time is short."

Hermas entered the house at once; nothing could amaze him to-day. His father lay on an ivory couch in the inmost chamber, with shrunken face and restless eyes, his lean fingers picking incessantly at the silken coverlet.

"My son!" he murmured; "Hermas, my son! It is good that you have come back to me. I have missed you. I was wrong to send you away. You shall never leave me again. You are my son, my heir. I have changed everything. Hermas, my son, come nearer—close beside me. Take my hand, my son!"

The young man obeyed, and, kneeling by the couch, gathered his father's cold, twitching fingers in his firm, warm grasp.

"Hermas, life is passing—long, rich, prosperous; the last sands, I cannot stay them. My religion, a good policy—Julian was my friend. But now he is gone—where? My soul is empty—nothing beyond—very dark —I am afraid. But you know something better. You found something that made you willing to give up your life for it—it must have been almost like dying—yet you were happy. What was it you found? See, I am giving you everything. I have forgiven you. Now forgive me. Tell me, what is it? Your secret, your faith—give it to me before I go."

At the sound of this broken pleading a strange passion of pity and love took the young man by the throat. His voice shook a little as he answered eagerly:

"Father, there is nothing to forgive. I am your son; I will gladly tell you all that I know. I will give you the secret of faith. Father, you must believe with all your heart, and soul, and strength in—"

Where was the word—the word that he had been used to utter night and morning, the word that had meant to him more than he had ever known? What had become of it?

He groped for it in the dark room of his mind. He had thought he could lay his hand upon it in a moment, but it was gone.

34

Some one had taken it away. Everything else was most clear to him: the terror of death; the lonely soul appealing from his father's eyes; the instant need of comfort and help. But at the one point where he looked for help he could find nothing; only an empty space. The word of hope had vanished. He felt for it blindly and in desperate haste.

"Father, wait! I have forgotten something—it has slipped away from me. I shall find it in a moment. There is hope— I will tell you presently—oh, wait!"

The bony hand gripped his like a vice; the glazed eyes opened wider. "Tell me," whispered the old man; "tell me quickly, for I must go."

The voice sank into a dull rattle. The fingers closed once more, and relaxed. The light behind the eyes went out.

Hermas, the master of the House of the Golden Pillars, was keeping watch by the dead.

IV

LOVE IN SEARCH OF A WORD

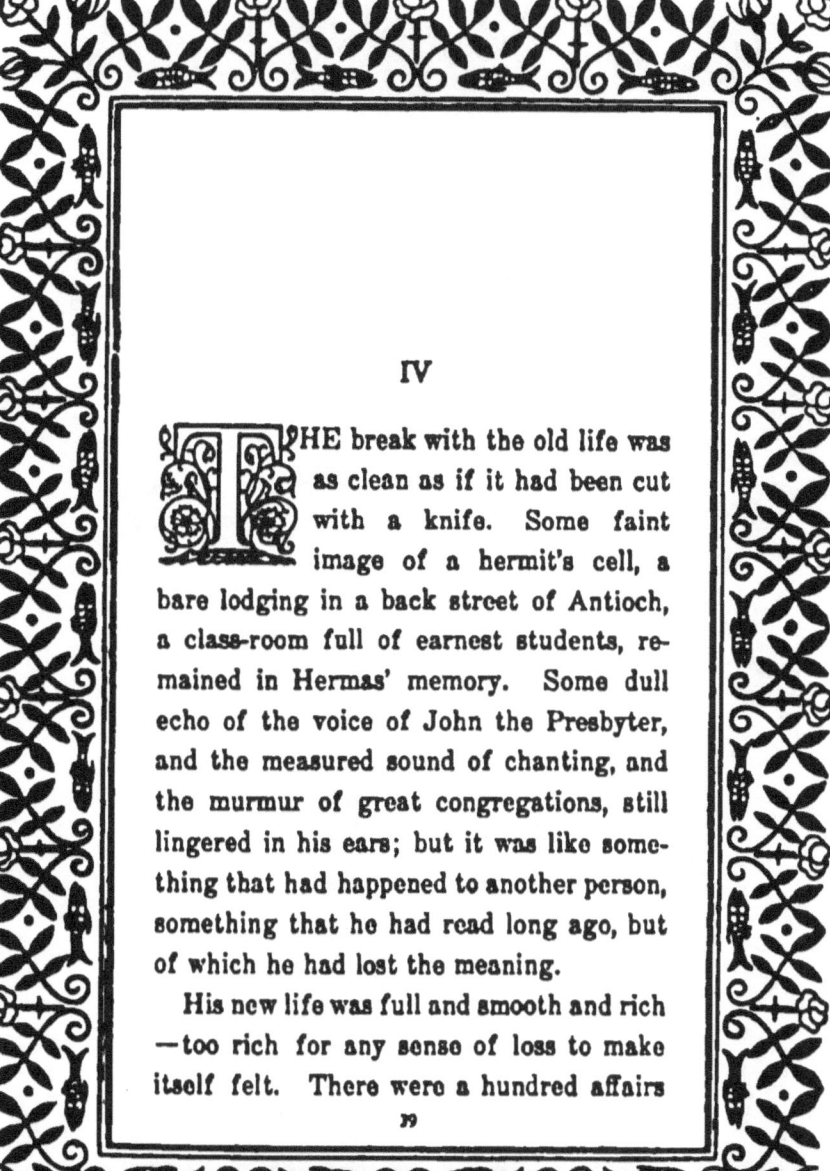

IV

THE break with the old life was as clean as if it had been cut with a knife. Some faint image of a hermit's cell, a bare lodging in a back street of Antioch, a class-room full of earnest students, remained in Hermas' memory. Some dull echo of the voice of John the Presbyter, and the measured sound of chanting, and the murmur of great congregations, still lingered in his ears; but it was like something that had happened to another person, something that he had read long ago, but of which he had lost the meaning.

His new life was full and smooth and rich —too rich for any sense of loss to make itself felt. There were a hundred affairs to busy him, and the days ran swiftly by as if they were shod with winged sandals.

Nothing needed to be considered, prepared for, begun. Everything was ready and waiting for him. All that he had to do was to go on with it. The estate of Demetrius was even greater than the world had supposed. There were fertile lands in Syria which the emperor had given him, marble-quarries in Phrygia, and forests of valuable timber in Cilicia; the vaults of the villa contained chests of gold and silver; the secret cabinets in the master's room were full of precious stones. The stewards were diligent and faithful. The servants of the magnificent household rejoiced at the young master's return. His table was spread; the rose-garland of pleasure was woven for his head, and his cup was already filled with the spicy wine of power.

The period of mourning for his father came at a fortunate moment, to seclude and safeguard him from the storm of political troubles and persecutions that fell upon

Antioch after the insults offered by the mob to the imperial statues in the year 387. The friends of Demetrius, prudent and conservative persons, gathered around Hermas and made him welcome to their circle. Chief among them was Libanius, the sophist, his nearest neighbour, whose daughter Athenais had been the playmate of Hermas in the old days.

He had left her a child. He found her a beautiful woman. What transformation is so magical, so charming, as this? To see the uncertain lines of youth rounded into firmness and symmetry, to discover the half-ripe, merry, changing face of the girl matured into perfect loveliness, and looking at you with calm, clear, serious eyes, not forgetting the past, but fully conscious of the changed present—this is to behold a miracle in the flesh.

"Where have you been, these two years?" said Athenais, as they walked together through the garden of lilies where they had so often played.

41

"In a land of tiresome dreams," answered Hermas; "but you have wakened me, and I am never going back again."

It was not to be supposed that the sudden disappearance of Hermas from among his former associates could long remain unnoticed. At first it was a mystery. There was a fear, for two or three days, that he might be lost. Some of his more intimate companions maintained that his devotion had led him out into the desert to join the anchorites. But the news of his return to the House of the Golden Pillars, and of his new life as its master, filtered quickly through the gossip of the city.

Then the church was filled with dismay and grief and reproach. Messengers and letters were sent to Hermas. They disturbed him a little, but they took no hold upon him. It seemed to him as if the messengers spoke in a strange language. As he read the letters there were words blotted out of the writing which made the full sense unintelligible.

42

His old companions came to reprove him for leaving them, to warn him of the peril of apostasy, to entreat him to return. It all sounded vague and futile. They spoke as if he had betrayed or offended some one; but when they came to name the object of his fear—the one whom he had displeased, and to whom he should return—he heard nothing; there was a blur of silence in their speech. The clock pointed to the hour, but the bell did not strike. At last Hermas refused to see them any more.

One day John the Presbyter stood in the atrium. Hermas was entertaining Libanius and Athenais in the banquet-hall. When the visit of the Presbyter was announced, the young master loosed a collar of gold and jewels from his neck, and gave it to his scribe.

"Take this to John of Antioch, and tell him it is a gift from his former pupil—as a token of remembrance, or to spend for the poor of the city. I will always send him what he wants, but it is idle for us to talk together any more. I do not understand what he says. I have not gone to the temple, nor offered sacrifice, nor denied his teaching. I have simply forgotten. I do not think about those things any longer. I am only living. A happy man wishes him all happiness and farewell."

But John let the golden collar fall on the marble floor. "Tell your master that we shall talk together again, after all," said he, as he passed sadly out of the hall.

The love of Athenais and Hermas was like a tiny rivulet that sinks out of sight in a cavern, but emerges again as a bright and brimming stream. The careless comradery of childhood was mysteriously changed into a complete companionship.

When Athenais entered the House of the Golden Pillars as a bride, all the music of life came with her. Hermas called the feast of her welcome "the banquet of the full chord." Day after day, night after night, week after week, month after month, the bliss of the home unfolded like a rose

44

"Take this to John of Antioch, and tell him it is a
gift from his former pupil."

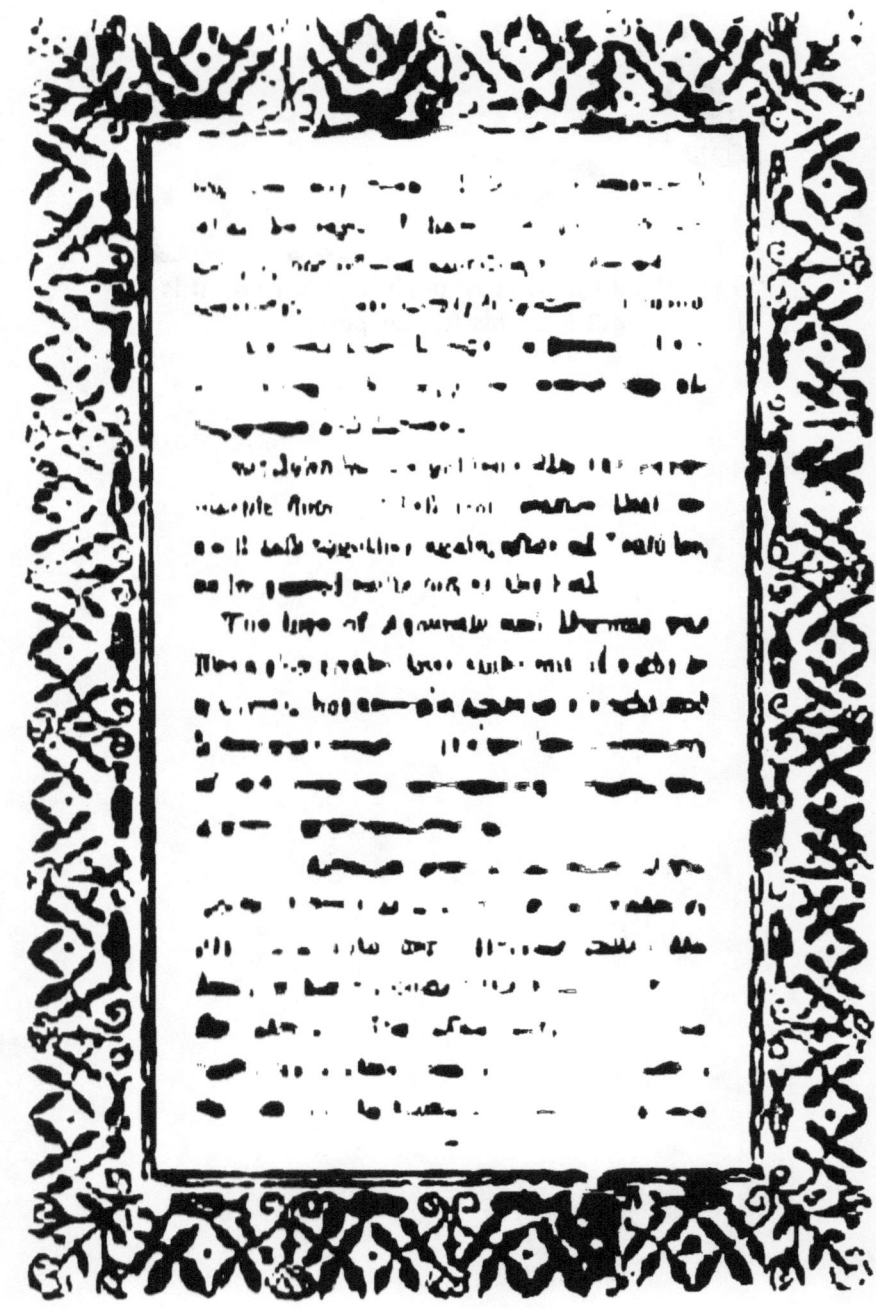

of a thousand leaves. When a child came
to them, a strong, beautiful boy, worthy to
be the heir of such a house, the heart of the
rose was filled with overflowing fragrance.
Happiness was heaped upon happiness.
Every wish brought its own accomplishment. Wealth, honour, beauty, peace, love
—it was an abundance of felicity so great
that the soul of Hermas could hardly con-
tain it.

Strangely enough, it began to press upon
him, to trouble him with the very excess of
joy. He felt as if there were something yet
needed to complete and secure it all. There
was an urgency within him, a longing to
find some outlet for his feelings, he knew
not how—some expression and culmination
of his happiness, he knew not what.

Under his joyous demeanour a secret fire
of restlessness began to burn—an expectancy of something yet to come which should
put the touch of perfection on his life. He
spoke of it to Athenais, as they sat together,
one summer evening, in a bower of jasmine,

with their boy playing at their feet. There had been music in the garden; but now the singers and lute-players had withdrawn, leaving the master and mistress alone in the lingering twilight, tremulous with inarticulate melody of unseen birds. There was a secret voice in the hour seeking vainly for utterance—a word waiting to be spoken at the centre of the charm.

"How deep is our happiness, my beloved!" said Hermas ; "deeper than the sea that slumbers yonder, below the city. And yet I feel it is not quite full and perfect. There is a depth of joy that we have not yet known —a repose of happiness that is still beyond us. What is it? I have no superstitious fears, like the king who cast his signet-ring into the sea because he dreaded that some secret vengeance would fall on his unbroken good fortune. That was an idle terror. But there is something that oppresses me like an invisible burden. There is something still undone, unspoken, unfelt— something that we need to complete everything. Have you not felt it, too? Can you not lead me to it?"

"Yes," she answered, lifting her eyes to his face; "I, too, have felt it, Hermas, this burden, this need, this unsatisfied longing. I think I know what it means. It is gratitude—the language of the heart, the music of happiness. There is no perfect joy without gratitude. But we have never learned it, and the want of it troubles us. It is like being dumb with a heart full of love. We must find the word for it, and say it together. Then we shall be perfectly joined in perfect joy. Come, my dear lord, let us take the boy with us, and give thanks."

Hermas lifted the child in his arms, and turned with Athenais into the depth of the garden. There was a dismantled shrine of some forgotten fashion of worship half hidden among the luxuriant flowers. A fallen image lay beside it, face downward in the grass. They stood there, hand in hand, the boy drowsily resting on his

47

father's shoulder—a threefold harmony of strength and beauty and innocence.

Silently the roseate light caressed the tall spires of the cypress-trees; silently the shadows gathered at their feet; silently the crystal stars looked out from the deepening arch of heaven. The very breath of being paused. It was the hour of culmination, the supreme moment of felicity waiting for its crown. The tones of Hermas were clear and low as he began, half speaking and half chanting, in the rhythm of an ancient song:

"Fair is the world, the sea, the sky, the double kingdom of day and night, in the glow of morning, in the shadow of evening, and under the dripping light of stars.

"Fairer still is life in our breasts, with its manifold music and meaning, with its wonder of seeing and hearing and feeling and knowing and being.

"Fairer and still more fair is love, that draws us together, mingles our lives in its flow, and bears them along like a river,

48

strong and clear and swift, reflecting the stars in its bosom.

"Wide is our world; we are rich; we have all things. Life is abundant within us—a measureless deep. Deepest of all is our love, and it longs to speak.

"Come, thou final word! Come, thou crown of speech! Come, thou charm of peace! Open the gates of our hearts. Lift the weight of our joy and bear it upward.

"For all good gifts, for all perfect gifts, for love, for life, for the world, we praise, we bless, we thank—"

As a soaring bird, struck by an arrow, falls headlong from the sky, so the song of Hermas fell. At the end of his flight of gratitude there was nothing—a blank, a hollow space.

He looked for a face, and saw a void. He sought for a hand, and clasped vacancy. His heart was throbbing and swelling with passion; the bell swung to and fro within him, beating from side to side as if it would burst; but not a single note came from it. All the fulness of his feeling, that had risen upward like a living fountain, fell back from the empty sky, as cold as snow, as hard as hail, frozen and dead. There was no meaning in his happiness. No one had sent it to him. There was no one to thank for it. His felicity was a closed circle, a wall of eternal ice.

"Let us go back," he said sadly to Athenais; "the child is heavy upon my shoulder. We will lay him to sleep, and go into the library. The air grows chilly. We were mistaken. The gratitude of life is only a dream. There is no one to thank."

And in the garden it was already night.

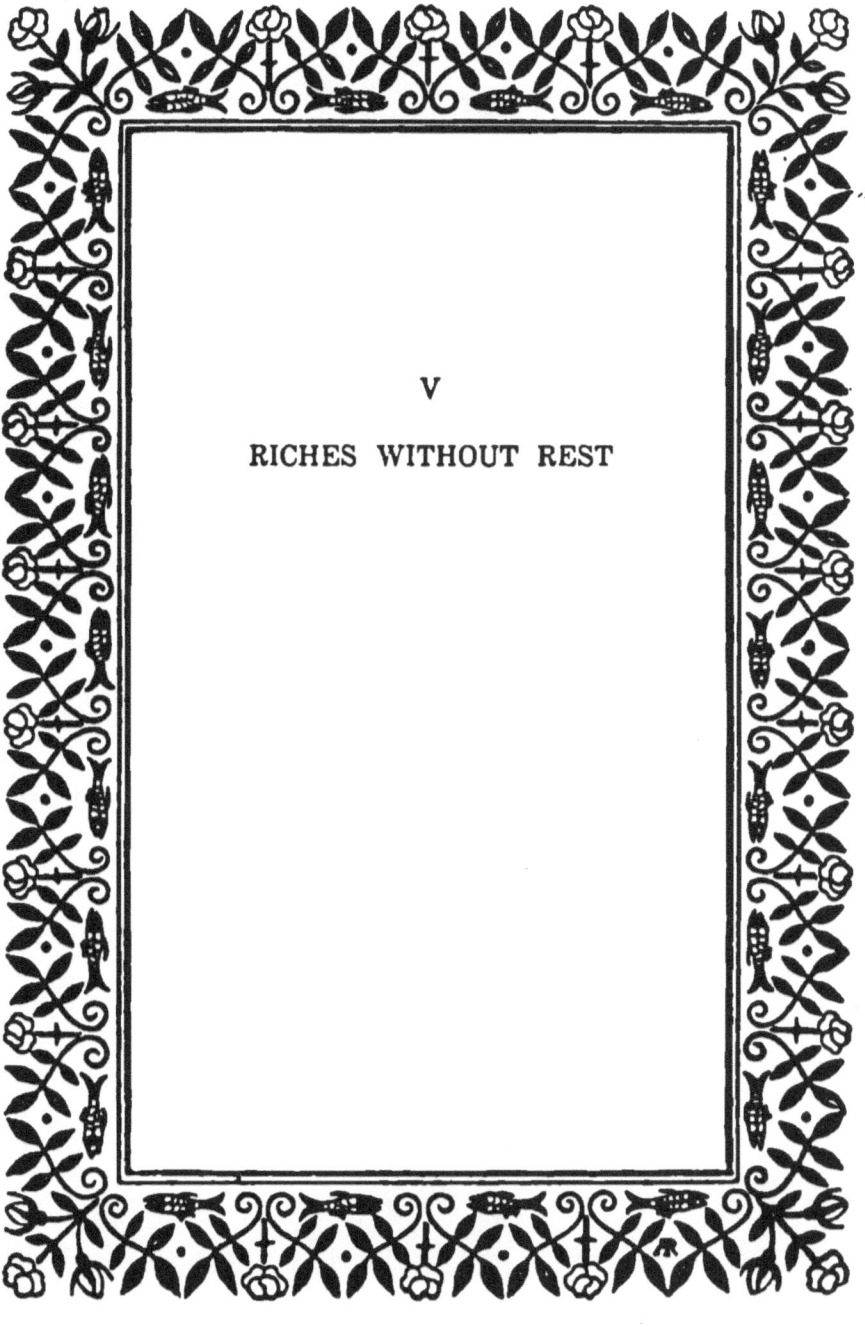

V

RICHES WITHOUT REST

V

NO outward change came to the House of the Golden Pillars. Everything moved as smoothly, as delicately, as prosperously, as before. But inwardly there was a subtle, inexplicable transformation. A vague discontent, a final and inevitable sense of incompleteness, overshadowed existence from that night when Hermas realized that his joy could never go beyond itself.

The next morning the old man whom he had seen in the Grove of Daphne, but never since, appeared mysteriously at the door of the house, as if he had been sent for, and entered, to dwell there like an invited guest.

Hermas could not but make him welcome,

and at first he tried to regard him with reverence and affection as the one through whom fortune had come. But it was impossible. There was a chill in the inscrutable smile of Marcion, as he called himself, that seemed to mock at reverence. He was in the house as one watching a strange experiment—tranquil, interested, ready to supply anything that might be needed for its completion, but thoroughly indifferent to the feelings of the subject; an anatomist of life, looking curiously to see how long it would continue, and how it would behave, after the heart had been removed.

In his presence Hermas was conscious of a certain irritation, a resentful anger against the calm, frigid scrutiny of the eyes that followed him everywhere, like a pair of spies, peering out over the smiling mouth and the long white beard.

"Why do you look at me so curiously?" asked Hermas, one morning, as they sat together in the library. "Do you see anything strange in me?"

54

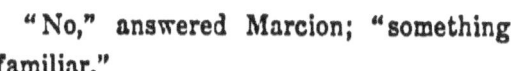

"No," answered Marcion; "something familiar."

"And what is that?"

"A singular likeness to a discontented young man that I met some years ago in the Grove of Daphne."

"But why should that interest you? Surely it was to be expected."

"A thing that we expect often surprises us when we see it. Besides, my curiosity is piqued. I suspect you of keeping a secret from me."

"You are jesting with me. There is nothing in my life that you do not know. What is the secret?"

"Nothing more than the wish to have one. You are growing tired of your bargain. The game wearies you. That is foolish. Do you want to try a new part?"

The question was like a mirror upon which one comes suddenly in a half-lighted room. A quick illumination falls on it, and the passer-by is startled by the look of his own face.

"You are right," said Hermas. "I am tired. We have been going on stupidly in this house, as if nothing were possible but what my father had done before me. There is nothing original in being rich, and well fed, and well dressed. Thousands of men have tried it, and have not been very well satisfied. Let us do something new. Let us make a mark in the world."

"It is well said," nodded the old man; "you are speaking again like a man after my own heart. There is no folly but the loss of an opportunity to enjoy a new sensation."

From that day Hermas seemed to be possessed with a perpetual haste, an uneasiness that left him no repose. The summit of life had been attained, the highest possible point of felicity. Henceforward the course could only be at a level— perhaps downward. It might be brief; at the best it could not be very long. It was madness to lose a day, an hour. That would be the only fatal mistake: to forfeit anything of the bargain that he had made. He would have it, and hold it, and enjoy it all to the full. The world might have nothing better to give than it had already given; but surely it had many things that were new to bestow upon him, and Marcion should help him to find them.

Under his learned counsel the House of the Golden Pillars took on a new magnificence. Artists were brought from Corinth and Rome and Byzantium to adorn it with splendour. Its fame glittered around the world. Banquets of incredible luxury drew the most celebrated guests into its triclinium, and filled them with envious admiration. The bees swarmed and buzzed about the golden hive. The human insects, gorgeous moths of pleasure and greedy flies of appetite, parasites and flatterers and crowds of inquisitive idlers, danced and fluttered in the dazzling light that surrounded Hermas.

Everything that he touched prospered. He bought a tract of land in the Caucasus, and emeralds were discovered among the mountains. He sent a fleet of wheat-ships to Italy, and the price of grain doubled while it was on the way. He sought political favour with the emperor, and was rewarded with the governorship of the city. His name was a word to conjure with.

The beauty of Athenais lost nothing with the passing seasons, but grew more perfect, even under the inexplicable shade of dissatisfaction that sometimes veiled it as a translucent cloud that passes before the full moon. "Fair as the wife of Hermas" was a proverb in Antioch; and soon men began to add to it, "Beautiful as the son of Hermas"; for the child developed swiftly in that favouring clime. At nine years of age he was straight and strong, firm of limb and clear of eye. His brown head was on a level with his father's heart. He was the jewel of the House of the Golden Pillars; the pride of Hermas, the new Fortunatus.

That year another drop of success fell

When Hermas turned to look he was lying like a broken flower in the sand.

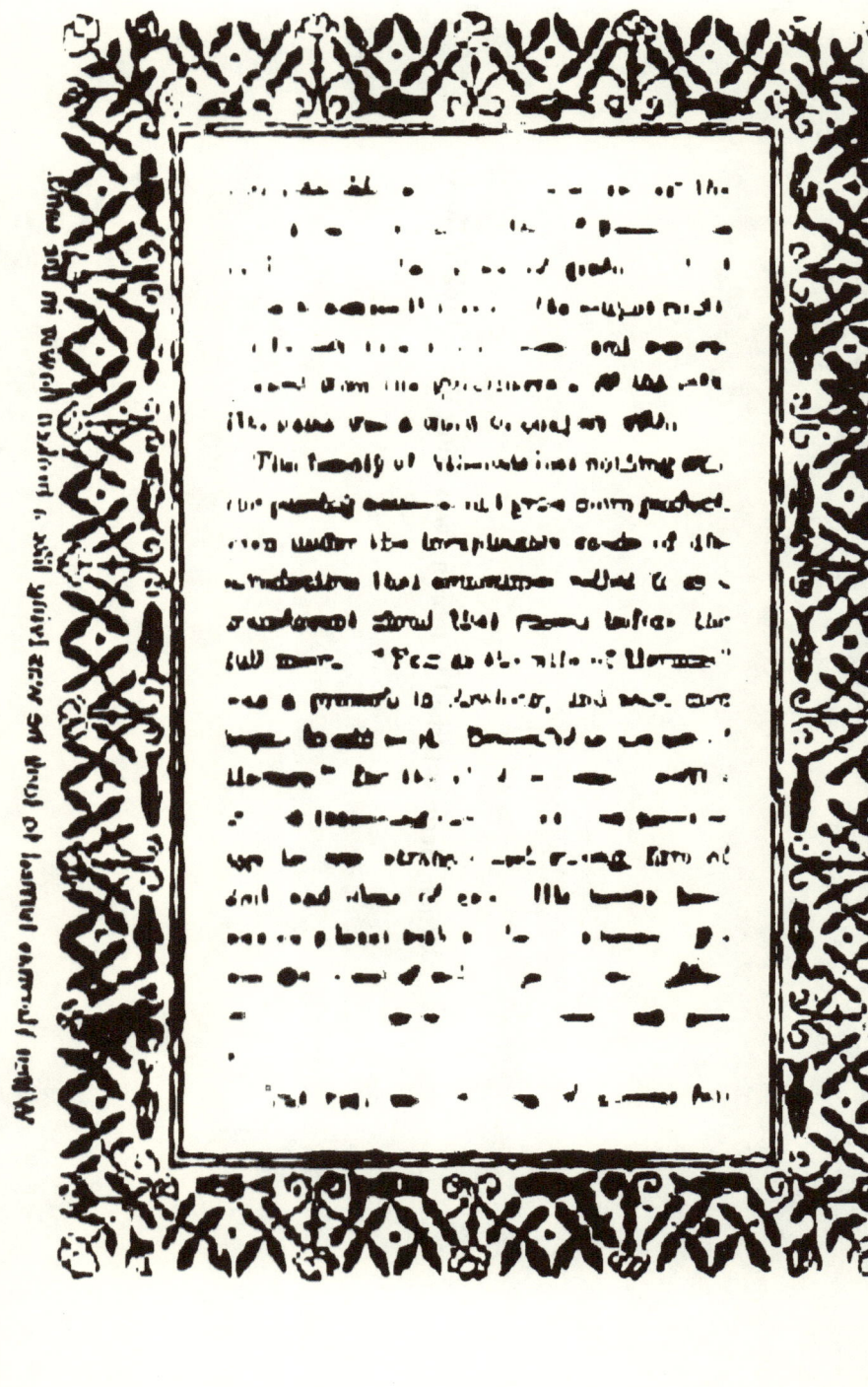

into his brimming cup. His black Numidian horses, which he had been training for three years for the world-renowned chariot-races of Antioch, won the victory over a score of rivals. Hermas received the prize carelessly from the judge's hands, and turned to drive once more around the circus, to show himself to the people. He lifted the eager boy into the chariot beside him to share his triumph.

Here, indeed, was the glory of his life — this matchless son, his brighter counterpart carved in breathing ivory, touching his arm, and balancing himself proudly on the swaying floor of the chariot. As the horses pranced around the ring, a great shout of applause filled the amphitheatre, and thousands of spectators waved their salutations of praise: "Hail, fortunate Hermas, master of success! Hail, little Hermas, prince of good luck!"

The sudden tempest of acclamation, the swift fluttering of innumerable garments in the air, startled the horses. They dashed violently forward, and plunged upon the bits. The left rein broke. They swerved to the right, swinging the chariot sideways with a grating noise, and dashing it against the stone parapet of the arena. In an instant the wheel was shattered. The axle struck the ground, and the chariot was dragged onward, rocking and staggering.

By a strenuous effort Hermas kept his place on the frail platform, clinging to the unbroken rein. But the boy was tossed lightly from his side at the first shock. His head struck the wall. And when Hermas turned to look for him, he was lying like a broken flower on the sand.

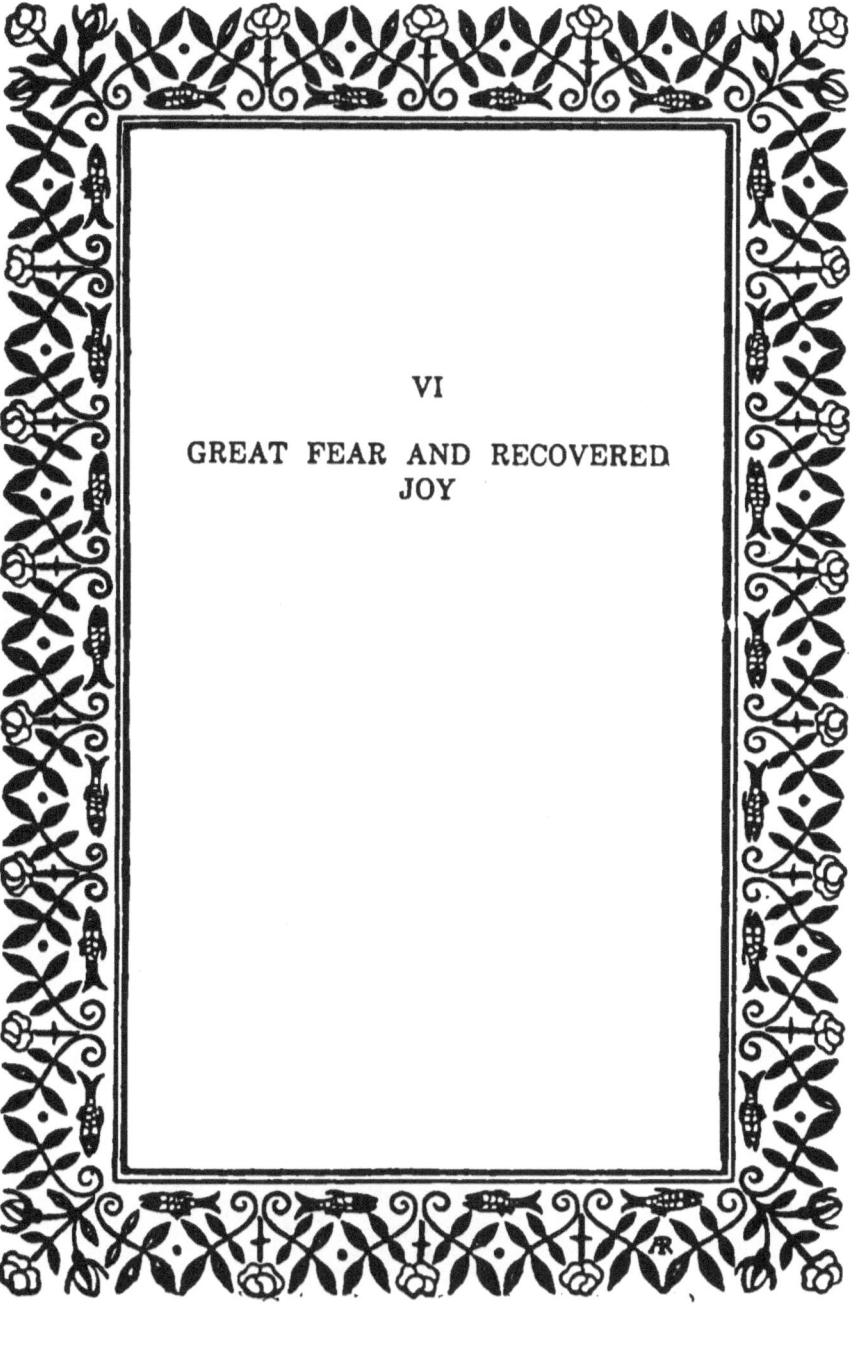

VI

GREAT FEAR AND RECOVERED
JOY

VI

THEY carried the boy in a litter to the House of the Golden Pillars, summoning the most skilful physician of Antioch to attend him. For hours the child was as quiet as death. Hermas watched the white eyelids, folded close like lily-buds at night, even as one watches for the morning. At last they opened; but the fire of fever was burning in the eyes, and the lips were moving in a wild delirium.

Hour after hour that sweet childish voice rang through the halls and chambers of the splendid, helpless house, now rising in shrill calls of distress and senseless laughter, now sinking in weariness and dull moaning. The stars waxed and waned; the sun rose

63

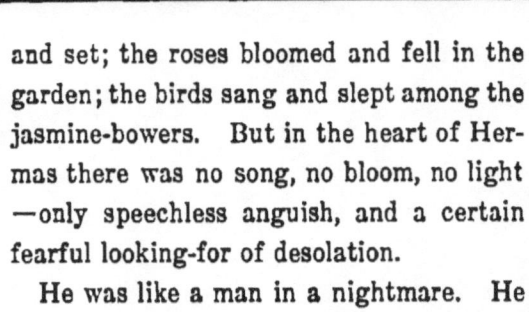

and set; the roses bloomed and fell in the garden; the birds sang and slept among the jasmine-bowers. But in the heart of Hermas there was no song, no bloom, no light —only speechless anguish, and a certain fearful looking-for of desolation.

He was like a man in a nightmare. He saw the shapeless terror that was moving toward him, but he was impotent to stay or to escape it. He had done all that he could. There was nothing left but to wait.

He paced to and fro, now hurrying to the boy's bed as if he could not bear to be away from it, now turning back as if he could not endure to be near it. The people of the house, even Athenais, feared to speak to him, there was something so vacant and desperate in his face.

At nightfall, on the second of those eternal days, he shut himself in the library. The unfilled lamp had gone out, leaving a trail of smoke in the air. The sprigs of mignonette and rosemary, with which the room was sprinkled every day, were unrenewed, and scented the gloom with a close odor of decay. A costly manuscript of Theocritus was tumbled in disorder on the floor. Hermas sank into a chair like a man in whom the very spring of being is broken. Through the darkness some one drew near. He did not even lift his head. A hand touched him; a soft arm was laid over his shoulders. It was Athenais, kneeling beside him and speaking very low:

"Hermas—it is almost over—the child! His voice grows weaker hour by hour. He moans and calls for some one to help him; then he laughs. It breaks my heart. He has just fallen asleep. The moon is rising now. Unless a change comes he cannot last till sunrise. Is there nothing we can do? Is there no power that can save him? Is there no one to pity us and spare us? Let us call, let us beg for compassion and help; let us pray for his life!"

Yes; that was what he wanted—that was the only thing that could bring relief: to pray; to pour out his sorrow somewhere; to find a greater strength than his own, and cling to it and plead for mercy and help. To leave that undone was to be false to his manhood; it was to be no better than the dumb beasts when their young perish. How could he let his boy suffer and die, without an effort, a cry, a prayer?

He sank on his knees beside Athenais.

"Out of the depths—out of the depths we call for pity. The light of our eyes is fading—the child is dying. Oh, the child, the child! Spare the child's life, thou merciful—"

Not a word; only that deathly blank. The hands of Hermas, stretched out in supplication, touched the marble table. He felt the cool hardness of the polished stone beneath his fingers. A book, dislodged by his touch, fell rustling to the floor. Through the open door, faint and far off, came the footsteps of the servants, moving cautiously. The heart of Hermas was like a lump of ice in his bosom. He rose slowly to his feet, lifting Athenais with him.

66

"It is in vain," he said; "there is nothing for us to do. Long ago I knew something. I think it would have helped us. But I have forgotten it. It is all gone. But I would give all that I have, if I could bring it back again now, at this hour, in this time of our bitter trouble."

A slave entered the room while he was speaking, and approached hesitatingly.

"Master," he said, "John of Antioch, whom we were forbidden to admit to the house, has come again. He would take no denial. Even now he waits in the peristyle; and the old man Marcion is with him, seeking to turn him away."

"Come," said Hermas to his wife, "let us go to him; for I think I see the beginning of a way that may lead us out of this dreadful darkness."

In the central hall the two men were standing; Marcion, with disdainful eyes and sneering lips, taunting the unbidden guest to depart; John silent, quiet, patient, while the wondering slaves looked on in dismay.

He lifted his searching gaze to the haggard face of Hermas.

"My son, I knew that I should see you again, even though you did not send for me. I have come to you because I have heard that you are in trouble."

"It is true," answered Hermas, passionately; "we are in trouble, desperate trouble, trouble accursed. Our child is dying. We are poor, we are destitute, we are afflicted. In all this house, in all the world, there is no one that can help us. I knew something long ago, when I was with you,—a word, a name,—in which we might have found hope. But I have lost it. I gave it to this man. He has taken it away from me forever."

He pointed to Marcion. The old man's lips curled scornfully. "A word, a name!" he sneered. "What is that, O most wise and holy Presbyter? A thing of air, an unreal thing that men make to describe their own dreams and fancies. Who would go about to rob any one of such a thing as

68

"Servant of demons, be still!"

that? It is a prize that only a fool would think of taking. Besides, the young man parted with it of his own free will. He bargained with me cleverly. I promised him wealth and pleasure and fame. What did he give in return? An empty name, which was a burden—"

"Servant of demons, be still!" The voice of John rang clear, like a trumpet, through the hall. "There is a name which none shall dare to take in vain. There is a name which none can lose without being lost. There is a name at which the devils tremble. Depart quickly, before I speak it!"

Marcion had shrunk into the shadow of one of the pillars. A bright lamp near him tottered on its pedestal and fell with a crash. In the confusion he vanished, as noiselessly as a shade.

John turned to Hermas, and his tone softened as he said: "My son, you have sinned deeper than you know. The word with which you parted so lightly is the key-word of all life and joy and peace. With-

out it the world has no meaning, and existence no rest, and death no refuge. It is
the word that purifies love, and comforts
grief, and keeps hope alive forever. It is
the most precious thing that ever ear has
heard, or mind has known, or heart has
conceived. It is the name of Him who has
given us life and breath and all things
richly to enjoy; the name of Him who,
though we may forget Him, never forgets
us; the name of Him who pities us as you
pity your suffering child; the name of Him
who, though we wander far from Him,
seeks us in the wilderness, and sent His Son,
even as His Son has sent me this night, to
breathe again that forgotten name in the
heart that is perishing without it. Listen,
my son, listen with all your soul to the
blessed name of God our Father."

The cold agony in the breast of Hermas
dissolved like a fragment of ice that melts
in the summer sea. A sense of sweet
release spread through him from head to
foot. The lost was found. The dew of a

divine peace fell on his parched soul, and the withering flower of human love lifted its head again. The light of a new hope shone on his face. He stood upright, and lifted his hands high toward heaven.

"Out of the depths have I cried unto Thee, O Lord! O my God, be merciful to me, for my soul trusteth in Thee. My God, Thou hast given; take not Thy gift away from me, O my God! Spare the life of this my child, O Thou God, my Father, my Father!"

A deep hush followed the cry. "Listen!" whispered Athenais, breathlessly.

Was it an echo? It could not be, for it came again—the voice of the child, clear and low, waking from sleep, and calling: "My father, my father!"

www.ingramcontent.com/pod-product-compliance
Lightning Source LLC
Chambersburg PA
CBHW032205010726
47493CB00008BA/2833